KU-679-309

Tintin and Snowy

Tintin, world reporter number one, is off to Chicago with his faithful dog, Snowy.
Watch out America, here they come!

Al Capone

The self-proclaimed "King of Chicago" doesn't have time for pleasantries: he just wants to get rid of Tintin once and for all.

Bobby Smiles

Villain Bobby Smiles is so sure of himself that he offers
Tintin a job in his criminal gang!

Mike MacAdam

At first it seems that hotel detective Mike MacAdam
has an amazing sixth sense for solving crimes, but it's not long before
the incompetent investigator bungles his case.

Big Chief Keen-eyed Mole

Leader of the Blackfeet tribe, Big Chief Keen-eyed Mole won't hesitate to defend his people against the enemy. Unfortunately he's been tricked into thinking that the enemy is Tintin!

The director of
KIDNAP INC.

The ruthless director of KIDNAP INC. likes to keep his trusty swordstick
with him at all times. Watch out: he's got a point to make!

Maurice Oyle

Maurice Oyle is a manager at the Grynde industrial estate. He can't wait to show Tintin around, but perhaps he's a little too eager to please.

TINTIN IN AMERICA

Chicago, 1931, when gangster bosses ruled the city . . .

Right you guys, listen, and listen good . . . Tintin, world reporter number one is coming here to clean up. That's tough on us, and I'm not kidding! He busted my diamond racket in the Congo and landed my pals in the cooler . . . So here's the score: not one single day does he spend in Chicago . . . OK?

Here we are, Snowy! . . . Chicago!

We'll go straight to the hotel.

Watch out, Chicago, here we come!

The Osborne Hotel, please . . .

There you go!

SLAM

Shutters down! . . . Sucker's walked right into the trap!

Hey, what's the game? . . . we're locked in! . . . And these shutters are made of steel!

We're stymied then. Even I can't chew through those!

BANG

CHICAGO 10 MILES

A blow-out! That's all I need!

Come on, come on! . . . I gotta hurry up . . .

All fixed . . . I'll still make it in time . . .

Have a good trip! Lucky I packed the right kit . . . He'll go through the roof when he finds I cut my way out!

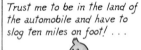

Trust me to be in the land of the automobile and have to slog ten miles on foot! . . .

CHICAGO 10 MILES

We're in luck! Here comes a police patrol . . .

Quick, can you catch that car you just passed, and arrest the driver? He tried to kidnap me!

Just keep still, Snowy, and don't be frightened . . .

This way we'll soon overtake that gangster!

That the car you mean?

Yes, it's him all right!

STOP!

Hands up, buddy!

You kidnapped me! Come on . . . Why?

They promised me five hundred bucks . . . They told me, if I got you into the taxi . . . dropped the steel shutters . . . and delivered you to the place they fixed . . .

What place?

The rendezvous . . . where I was to drive you? . . . OK, just to show I'm not really a crook, I'll spill the beans . . .

?

Look! A boomerang!

Thanks.

He's grabbed our bike!

'Bye, suckers!

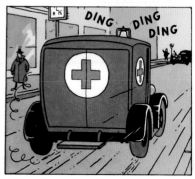

Holy smoke! . . . A real little tough guy! . . . He knocked out the boss, and Pietro too!

Good, he's gone! . . . I must take care of the other two before he comes back . . .

Whoops! There's one . . .

. . . and now the other . . . Both securely tied . . . The third man will be along soon . . . Ah, I can hear him . . . he's coming back . . .

Where the heck can he be hiding?

Watch it, Tintin, he's coming . . .

That puts paid to gangster number three. Now for the police . . .

Game, set and match!

Quick, officer, I've just caught Al Capone himself and two of his gangsters!

Sarge? . . . Send a car along. I just picked up a nutcase . . . thinks he captured Al Capone . . . and a couple of his hoods.

POLICE

Now what's the matter?

Ssh! Don't worry, Snowy. You stay here. I'm going to spring a little surprise . . .

Why doesn't he show himself?

At your service! Hands up!

Hello! . . . Front desk? This is Tintin . . . I need the police up here right away!

My dear Mr Tintin, this is a pleasure! I'm glad to meet you. Do please sit down . . . Have a cigar? . . . No? . . . Then I'll come straight to the point . . .

I'm Bobby Smiles, boss of the rival gangs fighting Al Capone and his mob. I'm hiring you at $2000 a month to help me bring him down. If you rub Capone out yourself, there's a bonus of twenty grand . . . Agreed? . . . Here's your contract. Sign there.

Get your hands up, you crook! . . . And I'll take care of that paper . . . Just remember, I came to Chicago to clean the place up, not to become a gangster's stooge!

So I'll make a start by arresting you!

Oh? . . . Is that so?

Marvellous little gadget, just under my foot!

I've been tricked . . . and now I'm trapped . . . Ugh! Smoke! . . . What a peculiar smell . . . It's like . . .

Help! It's gas! . . . They mean to kill me . . . Quick, my handkerchief!

Useless! . . . I'm done for! . . . I'm choking . . . My lungs . . . they're burning . . .

There he is, Nick! . . . O.X2Z gas sure does knock 'em out!

To the waterfront, fast. Lake Michigan for him!

No one here. All clear, Nick, bring him along!

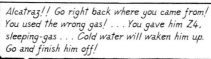

How about that, Snowy? Wasn't I right to keep away from the windows? Those dummies I used are peppered with holes . . . custom-made colanders!

Dead right! . . . It strikes me . . . Wouldn't it be a good idea . . . if those dummies did the whole job, instead of us?

Now they think they've disposed of me, I'm going to arrange a little surprise for our gangster pals . . .

Using dummies again . . . I hope!

Next morning . . .

Listen, Bobby, I just heard the Coconut mob are doing a job this afternoon, running a load of whisky, hidden in gasoline drums. How's about it?

Simple! . . . We grab it!

I've got a hunch there'll be a reception committee!

There! What did I tell you?

OK, come on out! Make it snappy . . . and no tricks . . .

Reach for the sky!

Hands up!! . . .

Get 'em up!!

You did a fine job, Mr Tintin . . . a fine job! Thanks to you, we've landed a really big fish, I . . .

Hey! What's that?

BANG BANG BANG

See ya, fellas!

Suffering catfish! Getting away under my very nose! And Bobby Smiles, too, the big boss!

Don't worry, I'll bring Bobby Smiles to justice!

A few days later . . .

These two telegrams are about Bobby Smiles. They say he's been seen in Redskin City, a small place near the Indian Reservations. Come on Snowy; it's Redskin City for us!

But . . . but . . . You don't really mean us to go into Indian country, do you Tintin?

Two whole days on the train! . . . Oh well, we're here at last, and that's what matters!

REDSKIN CITY

Just look, Snowy . . . A real Red Indian.

I have a feeling we look a bit out of place here, Snowy . . .

$5 $4

You wait here, I'm going to buy an outfit.

Redskin dogs! OK, so I'm a paleface . . . Haven't you redskins ever seen one before?

It's the very latest fashion . . . cartridge belt slung to the right . . . Last winter's models, all to the left . . .

Good. Just what I want!

The boss won't like this one little bit!

Boss! . . . Boss! . . .

Boss! . . . Watch out! I just saw Tintin in town. I'm sure he's come looking for you! . . .

Alcatraz!!

Meanwhile . . .

Yeah! I guess I have jes' the animal for you . . .

Aha! A wonder horse!

There, she's a nice quiet gal. Name of Beatrice.

Hello, Beatrice!

Er . . . A very fine beast . . . but I . . . don't really fancy . . . the colour . . . I'd prefer . . . a chestnut . . . or a bay . . . And . . . er . . . while we're about it, have you an even quieter one?

That suit you OK?

Yes, thanks. It doesn't seem quite so . . . fresh!

Right, Snowy! Lead me to the gangster hideout!

We've lost valuable time unravelling ourselves. It'll soon be dark now, Snowy, so we'd better pitch camp for the night and pick up the trail again in the morning.

We'll stop here . . .

Tomorrow morning we'll set off at sunrise . . . I'm determined that crook won't escape us again . . .

Just my luck! . . . Tintin will be here in the morning, and I'll have to skedaddle . . . They're going to find that tomahawk if it's the last thing they do!

Wakey, wakey, Snowy! On the road again!

Already?

Well, Chief?

Alas, Blackfeet still cannot find their tomahawk . . . It is lost!

What then?

What then? . . . It is quite simple: Blackfeet certainly cannot make war on Paleface. No tomahawk, no war!

Alcatraz and Sing Sing! . . . Dumb redskins won't fight . . . I've gotta get out of here!

The tomahawk!

?

Our tomahawk is found! Great Manitou wants war!

I sure hit the jackpot!

Great Manitou! Great Manitou! Give victory to your warriors!

Away! . . . To the horses! . . . Death to the Paleface!

Hello, here come the Indians . . . I tell you Snowy, if I didn't know the redskins are peaceful nowadays, I'd be feeling a lot less sure of myself!

Well, I'm scared to death!

What's all this? . . . It's an odd sort of way to welcome a stranger!

Whew! They've gone! Savages! Frightened me out of my wits!

Snowy, that was disgraceful! You abandoned Tintin.

Really, what curious customs you have!

Truly, Paleface does not have stomach of a squaw. He smiles and is calm.

But we see what he does later!

Face it Snowy . . . You've got a yellow streak. For all you know, Tintin's in danger . . .

Hear, O Paleface, the words of Great Sachem . . . You have come among Blackfoot people with heart full of trickery and hate, like a sneaking dog. But now you are tied to torture stake. You shall pay Blackfeet for your treachery by suffering long. I have spoken!

What sort of talk is that?

Now, let my young braves practise their skills upon this Paleface with his soul of a coyote! Make him suffer long before you send him to land of his forefathers!

But . . . he's crazy!

You speak well, O Sachem!

THWACK

Sachem, this little joke's gone far enough! Untie these ropes and let me go!

This Paleface commands us! . . . By Great Manitou, shall Blackfeet be ordered about like dogs? The Paleface shall die! I have spoken!

Resin! . . . That's an idea!

CLICK

PLOP

Oho! A catapult!

It worked!

Take that, pesky little papoose! . . . Shooting at me with a catapult! Do that again, and I'll have your scalp!

What a nerve! Behaving like that to Big Chief Keen-eyed-Mole, the Great Sachem himself! . . . Nasty brat!

Keep out of my sight for three moons, or else . . .

They shouldn't let papoose play with catapult . . .

PLOP

By Great Wacondah! . . . You too! You dare show disrespect to Big Chief Keen-eyed-Mole!

Me? . . .

Yes! . . . You!

Sachem! You strike my brother! . . . Browsing-Bison, he is innocent . . . He do no wrong!

22

Browsing-Bison's brother, he dare to strike Big Chief Keen-eyed Mole! . . . Death, I say! Death to Bull's-Eye, Browsing-Bison's brother!

Death to cowardly dogs who dare to attack Bull's-Eye because he defend his brother, Browsing-Bison, unjustly beaten by Big Chief Keen-eyed-Mole!

Splendid! Splendid! Let them fight. Meanwhile, let me get these ropes untied . . .

There! That's freed my hands . . . Now for my feet . . . Good . . . Move!

Now, who turned the Blackfeet against me? I must find that out . . . What about the gangster I'm chasing? Was it him?

They've stopped yelling and shouting, so the torture must be over. I'll go and see . . .

Alcatraz! . . . Over there! . . . He's escaping! . . . Knocked out the whole tribe! . . . It's impossible! . . . What a kid!

Help! . . . They're on my tracks!

BANG

I can hear shooting . . . I hope nothing's happened to Tintin!

No, it isn't the Indians! It's Bobby Smiles! . . . I might have known it! Now I understand why the Indians were so hostile towards me . . .

Snakes! . . . He's taking aim again!

BANG

Alcatraz! . . . What a drop! . . . The canyon goes down hundreds of feet . . . I can scarcely see the bottom . . .

Quick! Quick! I must save Tintin!

That'll teach you, smartalec! Meddling little busybody . . . I've got you out of my hair for good.

What's he looking at? . . . Surely it can't be . . . Tintin's fallen over that precipice . . . ?

And now, back to Chicago.

Wooah! . . . Wooah! . . . Wooah!

It's that dratted dog of Tintin's! . . . OK, he can follow his owner!

BANG

Wooaah! . . .

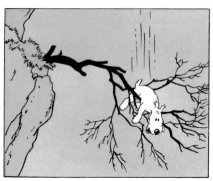

Hello, Snowy! We both seem to have come by the same route!

I fell into space, like you. It was fantastic: there was this bush, and I fell right into it. It bent and dropped me on this ledge. So here I am, safe and sound, instead of smashed to bits in the canyon.

Golly, what a stroke of luck!

Still, we're only safe for the time being . . . I can't see any possible way of escape from here . . .

What are you sniffing at there, Snowy? . . . Have you found something? . . .

Good gracious! . . . Amazing! . . . It looks like some sort of cave . . . Why don't we see if it leads anywhere?

Here goes!

Where are we?

Careful, Snowy! . . . Don't take any chances!

It's heading upwards more and more . . .

Where are we going to come out?

Look! A huge gallery, decorated with Indian paintings . . .

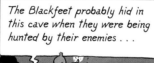

The Blackfeet probably hid in this cave when they were being hunted by their enemies . . .

This is the other exit . . .

Still going upwards! . . . Where can this tunnel be leading?

Ah, now it's starting to go down . . .

. . . then it's taking us up again, steeply . . .

I've got shot of that no-good reporter at last! Now, before I hit the trail again, I'll have some food . . . Too bad you're missing this, Tintin!

Hey, what goes on around here? Must be an earthquake! The ground's shaking under me . . .

Whew! What a weight!

Help! Help! It's a ghost! It's Tintin!

Well, well! What a coincidence! I must say, he didn't seem terribly pleased to see me again!

How very thoughtful of him to cook me a nice little meal. I really am extremely grateful for his generosity . . . To tell the truth, I'm absolutely starving . . .

M-m-m! Me too!

Sachem! . . . Sachem! . . . I've seen a ghost! The ghost of the young Paleface! . . . He was dead. I swear it! I hit him with a bullet and he fell into the canyon . . . Now he's just risen out of the ground!

What did you say? . . . Out of the ground? . . . He must have discovered secret of our cave! Take us there, O Paleface. We must finish this young coyote!

It's about two miles . . .

By Great Manitou, I will have his scalp for my wigwam!

Paleface-with-eyes-of-the-Moon, he has stomach of a squaw!

WHEEE

Little worm . . . he escape us!

Then you'd better get after him!

Come! Let my young braves follow their Chief!

Get on with it! Faster! Faster! . . . Good grief, anyone'd think you were scared to follow your boss!

Over ten minutes since they went down. I wonder what's happening . . .

At last! There you are! . . . Well?

Great Wacondah has sent victory to his braves! Little Paleface is vanquished.

Our great Sachem did the deed. He brings his victim . . .

Fine! Fine! . . .

Yet again Big Chief Keen-eyed-Mole, he is worthy of his name. After heap big battle in darkness, with help of Great Wacondah, I, Sachem of Blackfeet, conquer the Paleface. Let my young warriors drag him from hole!

See! . . . Pestilential prairie-dog! He trouble us no more.

By Great Manitou! It is not the young Paleface!

Wriggling rattlesnakes! I made mistake! It is Lame Duck!

I have idea . . . Let us leave Little Paleface there, to starve to death in his burrow!

Do what you like, but get rid of him! This has gone on too long!

This end, heap big rock . . . other end, sheer drop! What can Paleface do? No way out but death . . .

Don't be afraid, Snowy. We aren't going to moulder away down here. They think we're trapped, but we're getting out. Look I've emptied my cartridges and collected the powder. There! Now we'll blast their rocks to blazes!

You think it'll work?

You wait here, Snowy. I'm going to lay my charge . . .

Take care you don't blow us up as well!

Done it! . . . Now . . . there'll be a tremendous explosion . . . and that rock will pop like a champagne cork . . . Any minute now, we'll be free!

Hopeless! Not enough explosive . . . Now what? . . . I've no more ammunition . . .

Come on, Snowy, this won't do. We absolutely must get out of here . . . To work then! Let's try to dig another exit . . .

That suits me. But don't kid yourself we'll be out in five minutes . . .

That's it . . . Slowly but surely, we're making progress . . . We'll get there, Snowy, you'll see. Come on, another little effort . . . Hello, the soil feels damp . . .

You're telling me! . . . And it smells funny, too.

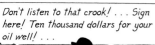

Out of luck again! With all that ballyhoo, Bobby Smiles managed to give us the slip ... How can I possibly find him again now?

CHUFF CHUFF CHUFF

Here we are like a couple of hobos watching the trains go by ...

Alcatraz! ... I think he spotted me!

There he is!!

Station-master! Station-master! What time does the next train leave?

Next train, huh? ... Tomorrow ... Same time ...

Beaten! He's defeated me again! ... Unless ...

Hey! ... Look! .. . Over there!

Jumping Jehosephat! My train's driving herself!

So long, folks! ... We'll send you a nice postcard!

Terribly sorry! ... I'm only borrowing it! ...

Hooray! We're catching up! I can see smoke from the other train ...

30

Slim! . . . Train's a 'comin' . . . Quick! Light the fuse or she'll smash into the rock . . .

Help! We're done for! . . . A huge boulder on the track!

PSSHH

BOOM

Boy, that sure was close! The dynamite went up in the nick of time! Two seconds later, and she'd have been blown to glory!

Leapin' lizards, Jem! . . . The trolley with our tools and the spare sticks of dynamite . . . It's there, half a mile down the track! . . . She's done for, she's a goner!

This is our lucky day, Snowy, and no mistake . . .

DYNAMITE
DYNAMITE

BOOM

Now then, off we go. With the supplies those good fellows gave us, I'm not worried about facing the desert . . .

In a small town, some miles away . . .

Yeah, that's all I know . . . When I came into the bank this morning, like I always do, there was the boss, and the safe wide open . . . I raised the alarm, and we hanged a few fellers right away . . . but the thief got clear . . .

After the robbery he got away through the window . . . Say, look at his footprints . . . a dead giveaway. See that: just one row of nails on the right boot . . .

With tracks like that, we'll soon catch him!

Madre de Dios! Thees footsteps, they geev me away pronto, pronto . . . What to do? . . .

!

Caramba! Un hombre . . . Oho! . . . Ees sleeping! . . . Bueno, bueno! . . . Pedro, he theenk he has a vairey vairey good idea! . . .

If he wake, if he move, I shoot heem . . .

Ees done! . . . Now, Pedro not have to worry any more . . .

Aaaah! . . . Up we get! Siesta's finished. Come on Snowy: on our way . . .

Hello! What an extraordinary thing. These aren't my boots. They have nails, and spurs as well . . . How very peculiar . . . I can't understand it . . .

It's really quite extraordinary . . .

Look at those tracks . . . I'd say he was trying to disguise them . . . But he can't fool us . . . We'll soon catch up with him!

Extraordinary . . .

Stop!

?

OK buddy . . . You're under arrest!

!

But why? I protest! . . .

You protest, huh? . . . What about the Old West Bank? . . . And the manager? . . . And the loot?

We'll be back in town by dark . . .

They're back! . . . They're back! They got the bank-robber!

String him up! . . .

Nothing we can do, Fred . . . It's a lynch mob! . . .

Heave ho!

Go on! Laugh! . . . It could happen to anybody! . . .

Meanwhile . . .

SHERIFF

Here are yesterday's facts and figures from the City Bureau of Statistics: twenty-four banks have failed, twenty-four managers are in jail. Thirty-five babies have been kidnapped . . .

. . . forty-four hoboes have been lynched. One hundred gallons of bootlegged whisky have been seized: the District Attorney and twenty-nine policemen are in hospital . . .

Hold on, folks, we have a news flash! We just heard the notorious bandit Pedro Ramirez has been arrested while trying to cross the State line. He confessed to yesterday's robbery at the Old West Bank . . .

Well I'll be a monkey's uncle! But . . . but . . . what about the other one? . . . Feller they're lynching? . . . Must be innocent! . . .

I jes' gotta save him! . . . No one's gonna say that the Sheriff . . .

Let 'em lynch an innocent feller . . . 'Specially since I'm the only one who knows he ain't guilty . . . Aw, now, one more glass . . . Las' one . . .

Git movin', Sheriff . . . My, ain't this whisky jes' delicious . . . Now . . .

. . . One for the road! . . . Jes' to give me strength . . .

Let's go . . . to stop . . . this . . . here . . . hanging . . .

Mus'n't hang around . . . Mus' get there in time . . . hic . . . to stop them . . . hic . . . wronging the hangman . . . hic . . . no . . . hanging the wrong man . . . Ha! ha! Ain't that a joke? . . . If I get hung up he'll be strung up! . . . hic . . . hee! . . . That's a good Hee! hee! one . . . hic . . .

An' I say . . . hic . . . the guilty ish innoshent . . . ish the . . . hic . . . the radio . . . No . . . ish the whisky . . . thass guilty!

VOLSTEAD ACT
WHOSOEVER SHALL BE FOUND IN A DRUNKEN STATE . . . PRISON . . . FINE . . . CONFISCATED . . . UTMOST SEVERITY . . . SHERIFF

Right, are you ready?

Gosh, Snowy, that was close!

Phew!

I can tell you, Tintin, we were nearly beans on toast that time!

We should soon come across the railroad again . . .

You see? There it is! . . . All we have to do is follow the track to the next station . . .

Are you going to play trains again?

When we get there we must try to pick up the trail of Bobby Smiles . . .

Chuff! . . . Chuff! . . .

I'm sure it won't be easy, but we'll manage somehow . . .

Hello . . . A sleeper across the rails . . right on the bend! . . . Somebody's up to no good!

No doubt about it . . . Someone means to wreck a train! . . .

Where've I met that scent before?

Very odd . . . No one about . . .

Oh my, oh my! What a surprise! . . . Our dear friend Tintin! . . . What brings you here? . . . Looking for me, perhaps?

Well, well! I'm glad to have spared you a longer search . . . By the way, I was planning to wreck the Flyer . . . A cool half million bucks in the mail coach . . . But on second thoughts, I won't bother . . .

No, I won't bother. I'd rather let the train go on its way. Big of me, isn't it? But naturally, I'll see you tied securely on the track first . . .

Now . . . What's he up to?

!

Snowy! . . . Snowy! . . .

Oh, no!

Vicious little mutt . . . like his master!

Monster!

Well done, Jake . . . As you see, Mister Smartypants, he knows how to use a rope . . .

So long, pal! . . . You have just fifteen minutes . . . to think about what happens to clever little guys who try to put the skids under Bobby Smiles!

I'm done for! That fellow knows his job: these knots are like iron. Tintin, my friend, this time you're finished!

CHUFF CHUFF CHUFF CHUFF

ALARM

What's going on? . . . Someone pulled the alarm . . .

Yes, it was me! . . . It is a disgrace! . . . I saw a puma attacking a deer. As a member of the American Association of Animal Admirers I positively insist that you do something . . . right now!

What?! Lady, you stopped the Flyer for that?! . . . Fifty dollars fine!

TRRRIT

I'm sure I heard a whistle . . . So I can't be dead . . .

HELP!

?

Now what's the matter? I heard someone hollering . . .

?

Smouldering smokestacks! You sure can thank your stars!

And how! If you hadn't stopped . . . I'd be playing a harp by now!

Next morning . . .

Now, let's have a look at the news . . . They should surely have found his body by now . . .

MIRACULOUS ESCAPE!
FAMED BOY REPORTER
CHEATS GANGLAND KILLER
From our Railroad Correspondent

Alcatraz! Back to square one!

Our dear Bobby Smiles will have quite a surprise when sees me reappear!

Oho, we're coming to the mountains . . .

Still a good fresh trail . . . quite recent.

There's a cabin up there . . . Can that be it? . . . What a superb hideout: a real eagle's nest . . .

Have we got to climb right up there?

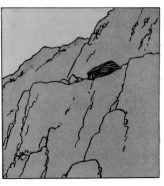

Aha! There he is! . . . Still on my tail . . . Never mind, that suits me fine!

We don't often go climbing . . . Good practice for us, Snowy! . . .

You know, Tintin, some people do this for fun!

Wait a minute . . . He's very nearly there . . . Now for the big laugh . . .

One . . . two . . . three! . . . Up she goes! . . . And this, Tintin, is one story you won't write!

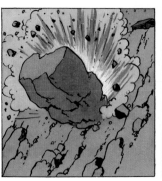

BOOM

Great snakes! He's got us! He's triggered off a rockfall . . . We're done for this time, Snowy!

I had to blow up half the mountain, but, boy, it did the trick!

Tintin, my dear departed friend, here's to you!

And to you, too!

Back from the dead!

Back from the dead, indeed! If I hadn't been protected by an overhanging rock . . .

. . . I'd be dead as a doornail!

Well, better late than never!

BANG

Nice shooting, eh, Mr Smiles?

Believe me, it's far better to give in. As you see, I always get there in the end.

Don't try any funny business!

Three days later, in Chicago . . .

Hello? . . . Yeah? . . . Chief of Police? . . . That's me! . . . Tintin? Nope! Not a squeak . . . Been gone a long while now . . . Trouble? . . . Sure is! . . . Nope . . . Ain't heard a word . . .

Come in!

PR   TE

RAT TAT TAT

Hello, hello! Reception? . . . This is Tintin! . . . My dog's been kidnapped . . . Yes, Snowy! Don't let anyone leave the hotel . . . What? . . . Your house detective? . . . Good . . .

What can I do? . . . What can I do? . . . If I refuse, Snowy dies! But give in to threats? Never! . . . So, what can I do? . . . What? . . . What? . . .

RAT TAT TAT TAT

Come in!

You're Tintin? . . . OK . . . Someone took your dog. Ransom. You're stuck, huh? Right, ain't I? . . . Good . . . See? Nobody can fool me for one instant, no siree! . . . Let me introduce myself: Mike MacAdam, hotel detective.

H-how d-'you do?

Mind if I begin detecting?

Right, here's the picture . . . Your dog's asleep. Someone comes in. Chloro-forms the pooch. Puts him in a sack . . . the kidnapper is thirty-three years and six weeks old. Speaks English with an Eskimo accent. Smokes "Paper Dollar" cigarettes. Wears an undershirt and has matching garters . . . Easily identified by a tattoo-mark on his left shoulder-blade . . .

The kidnapper has a slight limp with the right foot; cut himself trimming a corn the day before yesterday. And one more detail: snores in his sleep . . . When I tell you, sir, his grandfather was scalped by the Sioux forty years ago, and he has a profound dislike for birdsnest soup, you know everything I've spotted from a quick look round.

?

I'll be back within the hour . . . with your dog, of course.

What powers of deduction! . . . And what assurance! . . . A real Sherlock Holmes! I really didn't think detectives like that existed, except in books!

An hour later . . .

Come in!

Hey presto! . . . Your dog!

?

Monster! . . . You! . . . You stole my little Fritzy!

Ouchh! The good lady certainly didn't spare the rod!

The good lady? . . . What's all this about a good lady? . . . The attacker, sir, hit me over the head with a Javanese club. It was a man, twenty-two years old, with two back teeth missing. Wears rubber-soled shoes and is a regular reader of the "Saturday Evening Post".

You're . . . . sure?

Sure I'm sure! This time he won't escape me. You'll have your dog back within the hour!

Solving this case, sir, is the best job I ever did. You lost a dog? . . . One single dog?

Well, sir . . . I found you seventeen. And every one a pedigree pooch! . . .

Well done. Thank you very much. But we've already spent enough time getting nowhere. I think I'll continue the case myself.

Chicago Tribune! . . . New York Herald! . . . Daily News! . . .

Aha! The white handkerchief in the window . . . He's gonna pay up!

Give me a Tribune, a Times, a Herald, a News and a Globe . . . the lot!

Still nothing in the papers . . . That's good: means he hasn't called in the cops!

THE MOONSHINE CLUB

SPEAKEASY

BOOTLEGGERS TO THE WHITE HOUSE

OK, then? See you later!

See you later!

This must be the building . . . where they're holding poor Snowy a prisoner . . . But which apartment? That's the problem.

WOOAH WOOAH WOOAH WOOAAAAH

That's Snowy! Up there, on the eighth floor! That's his voice . . . He's howling . . . They're torturing him!

Hang on! . . . I'm coming! . . .

WOOAAAAAAAH!

???

?

All the same, I'm going to keep an eye on the building . . .

Careful . . . That's him coming out . . . Great Snakes! . . . Look, that parcel . . .

It's Snowy! I know it is!

He's hitting him! . . . I must do something!

If I dash round the block I can lie in wait on the corner . . .

A stick! . . . That's handy! Just what I need right now . . .

Steady . . . Cool, calm and collected . . . He's coming . . .

CLUMP

CLUMP

Oops! . . . Sorry!

Say, what's going on? . . . If I'm seen around here I'll be picked up for sure . . . Beat it, Bugsie boy!

Crikey, what a bloomer! . . . I'd better get out, and fast! . . . I'm in dead trouble if I'm caught!

BANG

BANG

THE SWORD
OF
DAMOCLES
ARMORER

You there! Yes you, baby-face! Come with me!

Here he is, sir! Little hoodlum!

Name and occupation?

Tintin, reporter . . .

You have to pardon me, Mr Tintin, for keeping you so long . . .

The trouble is, now I've lost track of the kidnapper . . . I'd better go back to the place I last saw him and try to pick up the trail.

This is where I hit that poor policeman by mistake . . . Let's see, I reckon this is the way he went . . .

Excuse me, officer, but have you by any chance seen a man in a cloth cap, with a large parcel under his arm? Somewhere here, about an hour ago? . . .

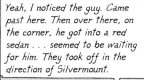

Yeah, I noticed the guy. Came past here. Then over there, on the corner, he got into a red sedan . . . seemed to be waiting for him. They took off in the direction of Silvermount.

KNIGHT BRAND CANS
Come in handy!

ILVERMOUN 15 MILE

WRIGLEY

COCA COLA

A red sedan? A red sedan just came out of those gates . . .

Could be . . .

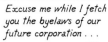

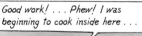

GOODNEWS
Senator
Kidnapped June 20
Ransom $100,000

M.R.C. SWORD
General
Kidnapped May 18
Ransom $100,000

SNOWY
Dog
Kidnapped June 25
Ransom $50,000

Snowy! . . .
Snowy! . . .

ped June 25
om $50,000

Wooah!
Wooah!

It's me, Snowy. Hang on just a little longer. I'm going to find the keys to your cell.

What happened? . . . Ooh, have I got a headache! . . . Yet I only had one glass of whisky . . . I wonder . . .

Hey! . . . Just you keep quiet for a bit!

Here I am, Snowy! You see, Tintin hasn't let you down!

Snowy! My dear old Snowy!

I never thought . . . I'd ever see you again . . .

KIDNAP INC.
RULES FOR GUESTS

Ssh! A whistle! . . . One of the gangsters upstairs must have raised the alarm . . . We'd better watch out . . .

That's a snappy outfit Tintin . . .

He's around here somewhere. I give you ten minutes . . . Bring him to me . . . bound and gagged. Now, get going . . . Scram!

. . . Number one reporter Tintin triumphs again with a gang of dangerous crooks handed over to the police . . . a kidnap syndicate busted by the young sleuth. The cops also netted an important haul of confidential files. Still at large is the gang's mastermind, now the object of intense police activity . . .

The object of intense police activity! . . . Ha! ha! ha! . . . The "object" is going to show what he thinks of your activities . . . He's got another card up his sleeve! . . . Hello? . . . Maurice? . . . Yes, it's me . . . You still with Grynde?

THE DIRECTORS OF
GRYNDE
HAVE PLEASURE IN INVITING
Mr Tintin
TO VISIT THEIR NEW PLANT

Well, well! An invitation to see the Grynde cannery. That should be extremely interesting. I think I'll go . . .

Correction! We'll go, you mean.

An economy measure to beat the depression . . . We do a deal with the auto-mobile plants. They send us scrap cars and we convert them into top-grade corned-beef cans. We reciprocate by collecting old corned-beef cans and we ship them to the car producers for reprocessing into super-sport automobiles . . .

Oh?

You see this huge machine? Here's how it works. The cattle go in here on a conveyor belt, nose to tail . . .

. . . and come out the other end as corned-beef, or sausages, or cooking-fat, or whatever. It's completely automatic . . .

Now, you keep right behind me and I'll show you how the processor works . . .

If you fell in there you'd be mashed in a trice by those enormous grinders. . . Look, down there, below you . . .

That'd be no joke!

Ha! ha! ha! ha!

TARD
EPPER
SALT
SPLATCH

(53)

Ha! ha! ha! Calls himself a reporter . . . and falls for that old gag! . . . The boss will be tickled pink!

Hello? . . . Yes . . . Ah, Maurice . . . You fixed it? . . . Good . . . Excellent! . . . What? . . . Corned-beef? . . . You're a genius! . . . How much? . . . Five thousand dollars? . . . Of course, right away . . .

Poor old Grynde! If he had the remotest idea! . . . Some of the things that go into his products . . .

What are you bunch doing, huh? . . . You guys got no work to do? . . . And who told you to stop the machines? . . . What's going on around here?

What's going on? . . . A strike, buddy, that's what! . . . The bosses cut the cash we get for bringing in the dogs and cats and rats they use to make salami . . . So no dice . . . get it?

Tintin!?! . . . Jeepers creepers! . . . A strike! . . . Surely it didn't start too soon? . . . The boss? What'll he say?

NO SMOK

Heavens, what an escape! We're all in one piece . . . If that machine hadn't stopped suddenly we'd be coming out of here in neat little cans.

I wonder how often they have that sort of accident!

Oh, my good sir! What a relief! There you are, safe and sound . . . I stopped the machine right away, but oh, how I suffered in those terrible minutes! . . .

. . . believe me, dear Mr Tintin, I most bitterly regret this dreadful accident. You have, all too literally, had an inside view of our business . . .

I was quite carried away . . .

It looks pretty phoney to me . . . The invitation, the over-friendly manager, and then that peculiar accident . . .

A nasty piece of work, our Mr Meatball!

Yes, it's me, boss . . . We're back to where we started . . . While I was calling you a strike blew up and they stopped the machines . . . I'm afraid so . . . Alive and kicking . . . But . . . What could I do? . . . I . . .

Bungling jackass! . . . Cut the sob stuff. You don't let a chance like that slip! . . . Sure! sure! At least I'll know in future that I can't rely on you! . . . That's all . . . As for the five thousand dollars . . . forget it!

Yes, gentlemen . . .

. . . our whole profession is on the verge of ruin. In a matter of weeks two of our most important executives, and many of their dedicated aides have paid with their freedom for the valour with which they attacked the enemy . . . Gentlemen, this cannot go on. Soon it will be as hazardous for us to stay in business as to live as honest citizens . . . On behalf of the Central Committee of the Distressed Gangsters Association I protest against this unfair discrimination! Forget your private feuds: stand shoulder to shoulder against this mischief-making reporter! Unite against the common enemy, and swear to take no rest until this wicked newshound is six feet under the ground! . . . I thank you!

Three cheers for the boss!

Bravo! Bravo!

You've said it!

. . . and so I raise my glass to our young and shining hero, a newsman as fearless as he is modest . . . who, with quiet courage, in a matter of weeks, has struck terror into the heart of every gangster . . .

I must say these official dinners are a bit of a bore . . .

You may be certain, ladies and gentlemen, that I shall take away unforgettable memories of my short stay in America. With a full heart I say to you . . .

. . . and to crown it all . . . I . . . hic . . . I've got . . . hic . . . hiccups . . .

MASTER SW

Help! . . .
Help! . . .

Wooah!
Wooah!

My goodness gracious!
What's happening!

No need to panic!
No need to panic!

Keep calm, please! . . .
I'm sure it's nothing
more than a blown fuse . . .

Look sir, there! . . . Someone
threw the main switch! . . .

?

It's unbelievable!
Gentlemen, Tintin
has vanished!

How disgraceful!

Hello? . . . Hello?
. . . Police? . . .
Tintin has been
kidnapped. Please
send your best
detective right
away!

Thank you for coming so quickly
. . . This is what happened . . .
Tintin, our guest of honour . . .

OK! OK! I already recognised
his dog . . .

Bring him back safe
and sound, and there's
another 5000 dollars
for you . . .

Within the hour, with
the aid of his dog,
I'll rescue Tintin and
catch the crooks!

You know something . . . it gives me the creeps out
here in the dark . . . Maybe I should . . .

C'mon Mac! Pull yourself together!
This is no time . . .

Funny
smell . . .

?

Golly! . . . It's fantastic! . . . Incredible!

Gosh, Snowy! . . . I must say, I never thought I'd see you again . . .

Tintin! Tintin!

Look out! Someone's coming . . .

Ha! ha! ha! . . . Hi! How ya doing, Mister Tintin?

You carried out my orders OK, Sam?

Yeah, boss. The dumb-bells are ready.

My clever little friend, I've got a surprise for you. We're gonna clamp this dumb-bell to your leg. Of course, it won't be all that easy to walk dragging this behind you, but then . . . ha! ha! ha! . . . you won't need to walk . . .

No! You'll need to swim! . . . Yeah! . . . Ha! ha! ha! . . . Great joke, huh? . . . See this trapdoor? . . . Down there, that's Lake Michigan . . . Get it? . . . Ha! ha! Ha! . . . Forty feet to the bottom! . . . we're gonna see if you can swim to the surface . . . You . . . and your dumb-bell, of course!

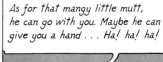

As for that mangy little mutt, he can go with you. Maybe he can give you a hand . . . Ha! ha! ha!

Goodbye, Snowy!

I won't ever leave you, Tintin!

Happy landings!

SPLOSH

And finish my report to our Association's members: I certify that in my presence Tintin the reporter was thrown into Lake Michigan with four hundred pounds weight on his feet . . . OK . . . Roll off ten thousand copies!

Sensational developments in the Tintin story! . . . The famous and friendly reporter reappears! Tintin, missing some days back from a banquet in his honour, led police to the hideout of the Central Syndicate of Chicago Gangsters. Apprehended were 355 suspects, and police collected hundreds of documents, expected to lead to many more arrests . . . This is a major clean-up for the city of Chicago . . . Mr Tintin admitted that the gangsters had been ruthless enemies, cruel and desperate men. More than once he nearly lost his life in the heat of his fight against crime . . . Today is his day of glory. We know that every American will wish to show his gratitude, and honour Tintin the reporter and his faithful companion Snowy, heroes who put out of action the bosses of Chicago's underworld!

LONG LIVE TINTIN & SNOWY

After a full round of celebrations, Tintin and Snowy embark for Europe . . .

Pity! . . . I was almost beginning to get used to it!

TOOOOOT

HERGÉ.

THE REAL-LIFE INSPIRATION BEHIND
TINTIN'S ADVENTURES

Written by Stuart Tett
with the collaboration of Studio Moulinsart.

Discover something new and exciting

HERGÉ

The scouts

Georges Remi joined the scouts when he was eleven years old. Scouting made a deep impression on the future Hergé, instilling a sense of loyalty, resourcefulness and duty to others that would later reappear in the character of Tintin.

During a camping trip in 1922, Georges Remi—known as "Curious Fox" to his fellow scouts—and friends from the Belgian Catholic Scouts Eagle Patrol dressed up as Native Americans. Many years later Hergé remembered: "I was interested in these people from that point onward."

about Tintin and his creator Hergé!

TINTIN

Coming home

Before they were published as books, the first few Tintin adventures were serialized in a children's magazine called *Le Petit Vingtième*. At the end of each story readers were invited to welcome the roving reporter back from the faraway countries he had been exploring!

© Acta - Studios Hergé archives

"Tintin" and Hergé
arrive at the Gare du Nord, 1930

Real events were staged for fans to attend. For the first homecoming event, a scoutmaster who wrote articles for *Le Petit Vingtième* suggested that one of his scouts, 15-year-old Lucien Pepermans, play the role of Tintin. On May 8, 1930, Hergé and Pepermans set off for the Gare du Nord railway station in Brussels, Belgium. Hergé scooped wax onto the scout's head to style his hair like Tintin's quiff! When they arrived at the station, thousands of fans were waiting to welcome Tintin home from his trip to Russia in *Tintin in the Land of the Soviets*.

THE TRUE STORY
...behind *Tintin in America*

When, on page 1 of the adventure, Tintin steps off the train in Chicago, little does he know that the most dangerous criminals in the city are already out to get him! But why did Hergé introduce the gangsters so early on in the story?

Once upon a time...

The first issue of *Le Petit Vingtième* was published on November 1, 1928. Although this was before Tintin's first adventure, Hergé illustrated other stories for the magazine. *Le Petit Vingtième* was the children's supplement to a Catholic newspaper called *Le Vingtième Siècle* (meaning "the twentieth century"). Hergé read articles about America in this newspaper.

Father Wallez

The director of *Le Vingtième Siècle* was a Catholic priest named Father Wallez. He distrusted American society and was appalled by stories of organized crime in the U.S.A.

Wallez liked the idea of a character who would expose corruption in other countries. The newspaper director wanted Tintin for the job. Hergé listened to his boss, and that's why Tintin's battle with the mob begins on page 1!

Once upon a time…

As it states at the beginning of the story, Tintin arrives in Chicago in 1931, "when gangster bosses ruled the city." But why were they so powerful? The National Prohibition Act, also known as the Volstead Act, allowed the passage of the Eighteenth Amendment to the United States Constitution—which made the production and sale of alcohol illegal starting on January 17, 1920. This was known as Prohibition.

Although Prohibition officers poured gallons of beer and whisky down the drain every day, there was a problem. Criminal gangs saw an opportunity to make money by creating an illegal trade—a "black market"—in alcohol.

Prohibition officers pour liquor down the drain in New York, 1921

By the time Tintin arrived in America at the beginning of the 1930s, gangsters had taken full advantage of Prohibition and started illegal businesses selling alcohol.

Prohibition protests

In the photograph below you can see members of the Women's Organization for National Prohibition Reform campaigning in 1930. Many people were disgusted with the criminal activity and violence associated with Prohibition, and they protested against the Eighteenth Amendment .

© Hagley Museum and Library

On December 5, 1933, the Eighteenth Amendment was repealed by the Twenty-First Amendment; it remains the only amendment ever to be fully repealed. Prohibition was finally over.

Native Americans

While Tintin battled away with Prohibition-era villains, Hergé had his heart set on other things. It was no accident that as early as page 16, gangster boss Bobby Smiles escapes out West. Now Tintin (and Hergé) could follow and visit a reservation!

Once upon a time…

In 1851 the first Native American Reservations—pieces of land managed by Native American tribal councils—were created in modern-day Oklahoma. Tribes were either invited or forced to inhabit the reservations, but often no attention was paid to the traditional links between the tribes and their ancestral lands. The photo (taken in 1923) on this page shows inhabitants of the Blackfeet Indian Reservation in the Glacier National Park.

Today there are roughly 310 Native American Reservations in the United States, covering 55.7 million acres (2.3 percent of the country), and there are over 500 federally recognized tribes. In 1971, Hergé visited the Pine Ridge Reservation in South Dakota. He was sad to see the once-proud Oglala Lakota tribe living in poor conditions that persist on many reservations to this day.

Now that we have a bit of background to this story, let's **Explore and Discover!**

EXPLORE AND DISCOVER

Hergé kept an archive of photographs and magazine articles in his office. The creator of Tintin was inspired by photos of skyscrapers, such as the one of the Channin Building on the opposite page. Just like many of the construction workers who built the tallest buildings in the United States in the early twentieth century, Tintin seems to have a head for heights!

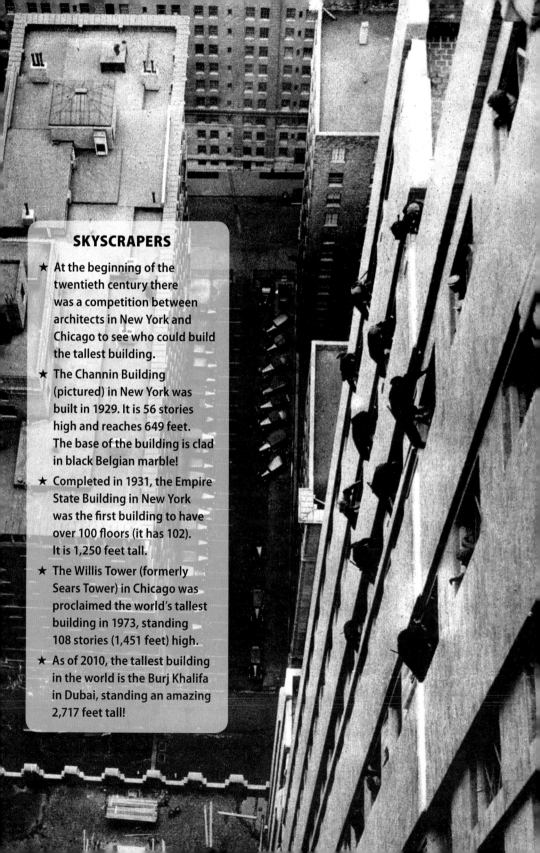

SKYSCRAPERS

★ At the beginning of the twentieth century there was a competition between architects in New York and Chicago to see who could build the tallest building.

★ The Channin Building (pictured) in New York was built in 1929. It is 56 stories high and reaches 649 feet. The base of the building is clad in black Belgian marble!

★ Completed in 1931, the Empire State Building in New York was the first building to have over 100 floors (it has 102). It is 1,250 feet tall.

★ The Willis Tower (formerly Sears Tower) in Chicago was proclaimed the world's tallest building in 1973, standing 108 stories (1,451 feet) high.

★ As of 2010, the tallest building in the world is the Burj Khalifa in Dubai, standing an amazing 2,717 feet tall!

COWBOYS

When Tintin arrives out West, hot on the trail of gangster Bobby Smiles, he wastes no time getting himself fitted out with everything a cowboy needs! He also acquires a fine horse to ride.

HORSE AND COWBOY EQUIPMENT

★ A western saddle is designed to be comfortable for the horse and rider: a saddle blanket (placed underneath the saddle) provides extra comfort for the horse.

★ The bridle consists of the "bit" that goes in the horse's mouth, the "reins" that are used to direct the horse, and the "headstall" that holds everything together.

★ A lasso is a loop of rope that tightens when thrown around a target, such as a bull. Lassos are made of stiff material so that the loop stays open when thrown. Real cowboys simply call a lasso a "rope".

INDIANS

When Hergé travelled to Pine Ridge in 1971, he had the chance to meet Edgar Red Cloud, the great-grandson of the famous warrior Chief Red Cloud. This Native American leader led successful battles against U.S. Army troops in the 1860s, but after visiting Washington, D.C., in 1870 he became convinced that his people should seek peace. He then worked to uphold the rights of the Native Americans during the development of the reservations.

Hergé meets Edgar Red Cloud, 1971

FEATHER WAR BONNETS

★ The image of a war bonnet instantly conjures thoughts of the Native Americans, but in reality only a handful of tribes—such as the Lakota and Blackfeet—actually wore them.

★ Traditionally every feather on a bonnet had to be earned by the owner. Feathers could be received for brave and honourable deeds.

★ Sometimes a member of a tribe would travel for days to catch an eagle, carefully remove a feather, and then set the bird free.

A NARROW ESCAPE

For several pages in the middle of *Tintin in America*, the heroic reporter is in terrible danger of being caught by the Native Americans. But the danger comes to an abrupt end when Hergé introduces a surreal sequence in which a city is built in a single day. Why?

BIG BUSINESS

Hergé wanted to highlight the plight of the native people he had been fascinated with since his days in the scouts. Despite their proud traditions and their fierce spirit, the Native Americans are no match for the ruthless oil barons in this story. Hergé's sequence shows how the expansion of modern civilization was eating up the land in America as it spread west.

> Here, Hiawatha! Twenty-five dollars, and half an hour to pack your bags and quit the territory!

> Has Paleface gone mad?

The next morning . . .

What's all the fuss?

Hey, you! Don't you know fancy dress is forbidden in town? . . . And keep out of the way of the traffic! . . . Where d'you think you are, anyway? . . . The Wild West or something?

INDUSTRY

When Tintin returns to Chicago, it's his turn to become the victim of big business…well, nearly! Hergé read about the Ford car factories (pictured below) of Chicago in a French magazine called *Le Crapouillot*. This inspired him to create the Grynde processing plant and food factory.

Le Crapouillot, October 1930

GANGSTERS GALLERY

Chicago's criminal fraternity is in shock at the news that Tintin has managed to outwit their colleagues once again! Hergé drew a hall full of villains at a meeting of the Distressed Gangsters Association. How do these guys match up to their real-life historical counterparts?

George "Bugs" Moran (1891–1957) was the real-life Bobby Smiles: a Prohibition-era gangster who had a rivalry with Al Capone. But when the Eighteenth Amendment was repealed Moran's illegal business dried up and he left Chicago. He was later jailed for robbery.

Hergé's official-sounding Gangster's Syndicate of Chicago may have been a joke, but in the 1930s, Charlie "Lucky" Luciano (1897–1962) set up the real-life National Crime Syndicate! In the end Luciano was not so "Lucky": he was deported from the United States in 1946.

Mob leader Vincent "The Chin" Gigante (1928–2005) began mumbling and walking around his neighborhood in a bathrobe, earning himself the nickname of the "Oddfather". But this was just a ruse to avoid prosecution for his criminal activities. The Chin ultimately went to prison.

George Kelly Barnes (1895–1954), better known as "Machine Gun Kelly", was a Prohibition-era crook who brandished a Tommy gun and robbed banks. He was caught in 1933 and spent the rest of his life behind bars.

THE TOMMY GUN

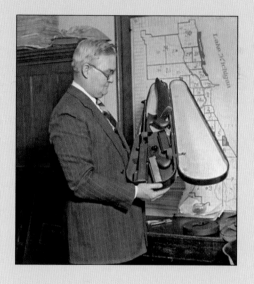

At one point in the adventure Tintin is nearly peppered by a Tommy gun, known in the 1930s as the "Chicago Piano". A gangster carries it away in a violin case. The photo on the right shows Captain John Stege of the Chicago Police Department checking out another suspect musical instrument in 1927!

With a life spent always looking over their shoulders, battling other villains and going to prison, gangsters only offer one lesson: crime doesn't pay! But although Hergé invented most of the crooks in his story, Tintin does come face-to-face with one real-life gangster: Al Capone!

AL CAPONE

Al Capone (1899–1947) is renowned for something else besides his crooked activities—he is also the only famous person ever to appear under his real name in The Adventures of Tintin.

In the 1920s, Al Capone rose to power as the leader of a criminal gang that became known as the Chicago Outfit. The gangster became so notorious that he was even featured on the cover of *Time* magazine on March 24, 1930!

Yet behind the scenes there was nothing glamorous about Capone's lifestyle. Shaken by all the violence, reportedly Capone once told a friend that he would never have moved to Chicago if he had known what his life would be like.

CATCHING AL CAPONE!

Tintin can't believe his luck—he has just caught Al Capone, the biggest fish in the Chicago criminal underworld.

If only the police officer would believe him! Unfortunately for Tintin and the good citizens of Chicago, Hergé had to let Al Capone escape to reflect the fact that the real Al Capone was still at large at the time he was writing this story. But not for long!

Sarge? . . . Send a car along. I just picked up a nutcase . . . thinks he captured Al Capone . . . and a couple of his hoods.

POLICE

ELIOT NESS AND FRANK J. WILSON

Eliot Ness (1903–1957) was the Chief Investigator of the Prohibition Bureau for Chicago. He dedicated himself to closing down Al Capone's illegal operations. Ness once teased the gangster boss by driving a convoy of trucks confiscated from Capone past the gangster's headquarters!

Frank J. Wilson (1887–1970) worked as a tax investigator for the U.S. Treasury Department. In May 1932, his investigation into Al Capone's undisclosed income from his shady businesses finally put the twentieth century's most famous criminal behind bars for tax evasion. In 1936 Wilson was made Chief of the U.S. Secret Service.

Nobody knows if Al Capone ever read *Tintin in America*!

DUMBBELLS!

Billy Bolivar bursts into tears—his wooden weights have been stolen. Ever resourceful, Tintin makes good use of the dud dumbbells. It looks like the sporty reporter wants to take the opportunity to do some bowling!

ARTHUR SAXON

★ Hergé was probably thinking of strongman Arthur Saxon when he created the character of Billy Bolivar.

★ Saxon—real name Arthur Hennig (1878–1921)—was a famous weight lifter nicknamed "The Iron Master".

★ Arthur Saxon mastered the "bent press", a one-handed weight lifting technique that Billy Bolivar attempts to emulate, without much success!

TICKER TAPE PARADE

What a wonderful send-off! Tintin is treated to a real ticker tape parade, a unique American tradition. Although ticker tape parades used to be held for visiting heads of state on special occasions, these days they are usually reserved for sports celebrations, the return of astronauts from space and military parades.

TINTIN'S GRAND ADVENTURE

When *Tintin in America* completed its run in *Le Petit Vingtième* magazine, it was published by Le Petit Vingtième Editions, a company that Father Wallez set up specifically to publish the Tintin books. *Tintin in America*, however, had caught the eye of a bigger publisher, Casterman. Soon the books would be published exclusively by Casterman, an established company with a wide distribution network. Tintin was going places!

Trivia: *Tintin in America*

Hergé sometimes made mistakes. On page 35, Tintin's boots change from one frame to another. Hergé also drew some of the cars with steering wheels on the right, but Tintin isn't in Great Britain!

The U.S.A. was still feeling the aftershocks of the 1929 Wall Street Crash when this Tintin book was published. Official records state 33 percent unemployment in 1932.

Although he doesn't get to relax in this Tintin story, Al Capone liked to play golf. This probably wasn't so relaxing for other golfers.

Today a gigantic enlargement of the original black-and-white picture of Tintin holding on to the side of a train (page 30) decorates a wall inside the Gare du Midi railway station in Brussels. Come and see for yourself!

The original cover for *Tintin in America* (1932)

GO ON MORE ADVENTURES WITH TINTIN!

THE SECRET OF THE UNICORN

RED RACKHAM'S TREASURE

CIGARS OF THE PHARAOH

THE BLUE LOTUS

TINTIN IN AMERICA

THE BROKEN EAR

THE BLACK ISLAND

KING OTTOKAR'S SCEPTRE

THE CRAB WITH THE GOLDEN CLAWS

THE SHOOTING STAR

ALSO AVAILABLE